Sam the Snowman

Susan Winget

HarperCollinsPublishers

SNOW SCHOOL
SNOW SCHOOL
SNOW CREAM

Sam the little snowman knows the secret of making snow is something called "the magic of giving." All the other snowchildren do it easily, but Sam can't even make one snowflake.

SNOWFLAKES
Fluffy
Icy
Frosty
Arctic
WINTER
SPRING
SUMMER
FALL
SNOW
ICICLES

One day his teacher says, "The children of Countryville are waiting for their first winter snow. I'd like you to help them, Sam. I know you can do it."

Down in Countryville, Sarah and her brother, Tommy, visit their friends in the brown cold woods. Everyone is wishing for snow so they can play when . . .

they hear a sudden **whoosh**!
Sam introduces himself and says, "I'm here to bring the snow," as bravely as he can. Sarah and Tommy cheer.

But Sam is having trouble.

"It's not working. I knew I couldn't do it," Sam says sadly.

Sarah and Tommy rush to comfort him. Sarah has a holly leaf for Sam's hat. Tommy gives the little snowman a scarf to cheer him up.

Sam feels so much better as he walks his new friends home.

The children's gifts have made Sam feel warm and happy inside. He wants to give them something in return.

He decides to try making snow one more time and raises his broom. Wishing hard, Sam gives it his **best twirl.**

And it works!

He paints the sky

and makes the woods and town sparkle.

Sam can't wait to share the snow with Sarah and Tommy.

They hurry to the woods, where the bears are sledding,

the birds are singing,

the foxes are frolicking,

and the skating is fine.

Everyone is happy on this perfect, snowy day.

Sam is the happiest of all,

for now he understands the magic of giving.

Sam the Snowman

For information address HarperCollins Children's Books, a division of HarperCollins Publishers, 1350 Avenue of the Americas, New York, NY 10019. www.harpercollinschildrens.com Library of Congress Cataloging-in-Publication Data is available.
ISBN 978-0-06-114475-2 (trade bdg.) — ISBN 978-0-06- 114476-9 (lib. bdg.)
Designed by Shira Cohen 1 2 3 4 5 6 7 8 9 10 ❖ First Edition